Saturday Morning Football

Story by Annette Smith

Illustrations by Richard Hoit

Contents

Chapter 1	Watching the Game	2
Chapter 2	A Goal!	8
Chapter 3	On the Field	12

Chapter 1

Watching the Game

After school on Friday,
Tom ran to meet his grandfather.

"Grandpa! Grandpa!" he shouted.
"Can we go down to the park tomorrow
at nine o'clock, please?
The six-year-old children play football
down there every Saturday morning."

"Yes," smiled Grandpa. "That will be fun."

The next morning,
Tom and Grandpa rode their bikes
down to the park.

Some boys and girls were there,
and they were kicking a ball around.

"Go and play with the children, Tom,"
said Grandpa.

"Not yet," said Tom.
"I'll just watch them."

Tom was starting to feel a bit scared
because he had never played
in a team before.
Now he wanted to go home
and play by himself.

Chapter 2
A Goal!

Some more children ran onto the field.

Tom stayed by Grandpa.

"Hi, Tom!" shouted Ryan.
"Come and play in this team with me."

Tom looked down at his feet.
He didn't want to go onto the field.

Ryan's father came over to talk to Grandpa.

Then, Ryan's dad said to Tom,
"The coach will show you what to do."

But Tom stayed by Grandpa
and watched the children.

Ryan ran very fast.
He kicked the ball hard,
and it went into the net.

"A goal!" shouted Ryan's dad.
"Well done, Ryan!
You scored the first goal."

Chapter 3

On the Field

At the end of the game,
the coach said to the children,
"That was a very good game.
I hope you will all come back again
next Saturday.
Ryan, this medal is for you.
You are the player of the day."

Ryan ran over to show the medal
to his father.

His father patted him on the back.
"Good boy, Ryan," he said.
"Now, the mums and dads and grandpas
can have a game against the children."

"Can I be the goalie?" laughed Grandpa.

"Are **you** going to play, Grandpa?"
said Tom.

"You bet!" said Grandpa.
"Are you coming, too?"

Tom and Grandpa ran onto the field.

"I **will** play football in Ryan's team
next Saturday," said Tom, with a big smile.